Sushi Doesn't Like Broccoli ...yet

Rylan H. Bender

Illustrated by Jasmine Smith

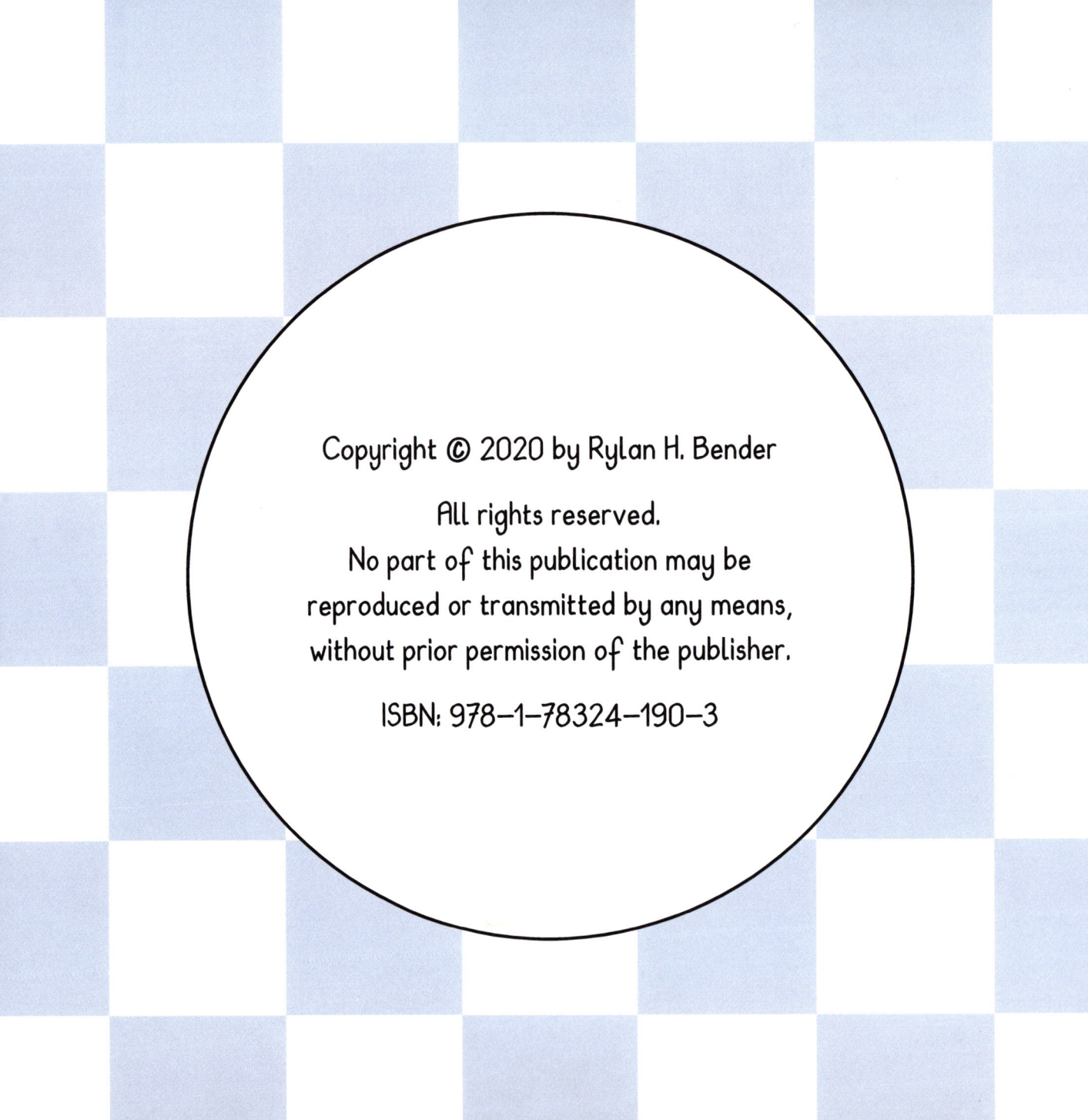

Copyright © 2020 by Rylan H. Bender

All rights reserved.
No part of this publication may be
reproduced or transmitted by any means,
without prior permission of the publisher.

ISBN: 978-1-78324-190-3

To my children Bear and Baylor,

Thank you for continually pushing me to be my best self. Know that you are deeply and wholeheartedly loved despite not liking broccoli. Keep trying. Small bites can lead to big discoveries.
Love, Mom

This is Sushi. He is a good dog. He loves to play and tug on his favorite rope. He loves to go for rides in the car while wearing his best bowtie. He loves his friends at the dog park. And he loves to eat his favorite food, chicken! But Sushi does not love to try new things.

No, no, nope, nada. No way. Not new things. Never.

Tonight seemed like a normal night. Sushi waited patiently for his Momma to toss him a piece of his favorite chicken, the same way she ALWAYS did while cooking his dinner.
But tonight was different. Tonight, she tossed him a piece of broccoli! Raw BROCCOLI!

"Go on. Give it a try," said his Momma. Sushi immediately became very nervous.

He had never had broccoli. He had never even SEEN broccoli. So he knew he had to be brave and try it.

On the first try, Sushi ran away from it and hid under the couch. This was obviously NOT chicken. It's GREEN! Yucky things are GREEN!

On the second try, he ran towards it as fast as his paws would carry him and... YIKES! He TOUCHED IT! It felt cold and rubbery. Not warm and soft like his favorite chicken.

On the third try, he barked and growled at it to show the broccoli who was king of the house.

This broccoli was not welcome here. Only his favorite chicken was allowed in his bowl.

On the fourth try, he nudged it with his nose but the smell made his eyes water, his nose squish, his tail wiggle, and his ears lay flat.

It smelled like something his Momma found in the back yard in the same dirt pile where he frequently snacked on mulch. It did not smell like his favorite chicken.

On the fifth try, he licked it. The texture felt more like grass and less like his favorite chicken, which he kindly reminded his Momma that he wanted as he barked and howled at her feet. Sushi was getting frustrated. He wanted chicken.

He thought about hiding under the couch and never coming out but that sure sounded awfully boring and lonely.

On the sixth try, he held his breath, quickly picked up the piece of broccoli into his mouth and launched it across the room, smashing it against the wall!

"SUSHI!" yelled his Momma.
"We do NOT throw food!"

This food sure didn't look or taste like his food. Not his chicken. Sushi was upset. Would he ever get chicken again if he ate the broccoli and liked it?

What if there was no more chicken at all? Or maybe, what if broccoli tastes BETTER than chicken? No way. That would be weird. But it's certainly possible.

After all, his Momma sure liked it! 'Maybe I should try it,' thought Sushi. 'Just a bite. Green is my favorite color. And I love the shape of it. It looks like a little tree!

It even bounces really high when I throw it against the wall.' Sushi laughed and barked and laughed and barked.

So, on the seventh try, Sushi slowly and carefully walked over to the piece of broccoli that he had hidden from, barked at, growled at, nudged, licked, and had thrown across the room. And he took a TEENY TINY TEENSIE WEENSIE little bite.

Then he took a medium size bite.

Sushi barked for a second taste test just to be sure it wasn't a hoax. His Momma was happy to oblige and gave Sushi his dinner bowl full of his new favorite; chicken with a side of broccoli.

And this time,
he promised NOT
to throw it
against the wall.

CPSIA information can be obtained at www.ICGtesting.com
Printed in the USA
LVIW011901050221
678195LV00002B/2